This book belongs to

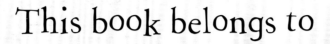

. . . .

. . . .

Written by Sue Nicholson
Illustrated by Capucine Mazille

First published by Parragon in 2008

Parragon
Queen Street House
4 Queen Street
Bath BA1 1HE, UK

Please retain information for future reference.

ISBN 978-1-4075-2165-7

Printed in China

My tooth is loose!

PaRragon

Bath · New York · Singapore · Hong Kong · Cologne · Delhi · Melbourne

Lily loved dressing up. She would dress up as a fairy …

a mermaid …

a cowgirl …

or a pirate.

But more than anything she loved to dress up as a princess.

She would put on her fancy princess dress …

her sparkly princess slippers …

and her bejeweled princess tiara …

and she would practice curtseys and fan-fluttering in front of her mirror until it was time for bed.

"Come on, Princess Lily! It's time for bed!" called her grown-up sister Maria one evening, "and don't forget to brush your teeth!"

"I'm far too busy!" said Lily, practicing her very best princess curtsey.

"Too busy to brush your teeth?" replied Maria, sticking her head around Lily's bedroom door. "Real princesses always brush their teeth, to keep them clean and healthy. That's why a princess's teeth are so sparkly. Don't you want a real princess smile?"

Lily took a quick look at her teeth in the mirror.
Was that a piece of spinach from tonight's dinner?
She raced straight to the bathroom, where she brushed . . .

and she scrubbed

and she rubbed

and she frothed

and she fizzed

and she rinsed . . .

until she had dazzling, sparkling teeth—just like a real princess.

After that, Lily took great care to brush her teeth every morning after breakfast and every night before she went to bed. And everyone agreed, she did have a truly sparkling smile. But one morning, when Lily woke up, something strange had happened inside her mouth.

One of her beautiful princess-perfect front teeth

was loose!

She leaped out of bed and crashed downstairs (not at all like a princess!) to tell Maria the terrible news.

"I'm NEVER going to be a real princess—my tooth is falling out!" cried Lily. "Princesses have shiny white smiles, not big holes where their teeth should be!"

"Don't cry, Lily," said Maria kindly, giving her little sister a big hug. "It will be alright. Everyone loses their baby teeth—even princesses!"

"Really?" sniffed Lily.

"Promise," replied Maria. "These are not your real, grown-up teeth, you see," explained Maria. "They're called your milk teeth. When they start to wobble and fall out it means that your big, grown-up teeth are growing underneath. Before you know it you'll have a proper grown-up princess smile."

But Lily wasn't sure.

"Oh, and then there's the tooth fairy!" said Maria. "If you save your tooth in a special box when it falls out, and put it under your pillow before you go to sleep, the Tooth Fairy will come and collect it during the night and leave you a shiny coin."

"I know all about the tooth fairy," said Lily sadly, "My friend Jake got fifty cents when he lost a tooth …

"… but I don't want any money," she continued with a sob,

"I want my tooth to stop being loose!"

"Princesses don't have loose teeth!"

Lily spent the next few days thinking of ways that she could keep her loose tooth—and her dazzling, sparkling princess smile.

"Jake's tooth came out when he ate a crunchy apple," Lily announced at breakfast, one day, "so I'm only going to eat soft, mushy food, such as bananas, soup, and ice cream!"

"You'll get bored!" warned Maria.
"I won't" said Lily.
"You'll get hungry!" warned Lily's mom.
"I WON'T!" said Lily.

But she did. Lily soon got bored of mushy food and she soon got hungry
and her wobbly tooth got **wobblier** and **wobblier**.

"THAT'S IT!" said Lily the next morning. "I'm never, ever going to brush my teeth again! It must be my toothbrush making my tooth loose."

"Well that's not a very sensible idea, Lily," warned Maria. "Your teeth won't be clean and healthy—and they certainly won't be shiny"

"And your mouth will taste yucky," warned her dad.

"It won't!" said Lily.

But by dinner, Lily's mouth felt horrible and her teeth lost their sparkle.
Nobody wanted to kiss her—not even the cat.

So Lily sighed a big, fancy princess sigh and went back to brushing her teeth.
And her loose tooth got looser and looser.

"I know!" announced Lily a few days later, "I'll just keep my mouth closed," "I won't talk, I won't laugh, and I won't sing. Then there's NO WAY my tooth can fall out."

"Oh Lily!" laughed Maria. "No one will be able to understand what you're saying, and you love to talk so much—it won't last! I bet you'll sing if your favorite song comes on the radio," said Mom.

"Mm mm mmm!" said Lily.

"I'm going to tell you one of my special jokes," said Dad—"that'll soon have you laughing!"

But Lily loved to talk and she did LOVE to sing and her dad's jokes were very funny (but she didn't tell him that in case he got big-headed!).
Lily couldn't help it, she was soon . . .

chatting . . .

warbling . . .

and giggling as usual.

And her loose tooth got looser and looser and looser.

"There's nothing else for it," sighed Lily, "I'll have to stick it in my mouth with glue!" exclaimed Lily.

"Don't be silly," replied Maria. "You can't put glue in your mouth!"

"How about honey, then?" said Lily, "or chewy toffee?"

"It will melt and get all messy!" warned Maria.

"It won't," said Lily.

But it did and her loose tooth got looser and looser and looser and looser …

until, one evening, the loose tooth dropped out of Lily's mouth! She took one look in the mirror, then burst into tears and ran to hide under her bed.

Maria came to find her.

"I know you're sad about losing your tooth," she said, giving Lily a tight hug, "but you'll always be a REAL princess to me!"

"Even with a gappy smile?" sobbed Lily.

"Even with a gappy smile," said Maria. "Look! I've got this for you to cheer you up."

She handed Lily a pretty little tin, with a sparkly pattern on the lid. Perfect for a princess.

"Don't forget to put your tooth in it tonight," said Maria.

"I won't!" said Lily, wiping away her tears.

That night, Lily put her shiny little tooth into the tin, and slipped it under her pillow. She shut her eyes right away and fell to sleep dreaming about tooth fairies.

In the morning, Lily looked in her tin and found a shiny silver coin. She ran to show Maria.

"Do you feel better now?" asked Maria.

"Yes," smiled Lily, "much better, and I've decided—I'm going to save up my tooth money for a sparkly dazzling, bejeweled princess necklace."

"You'll need another loose tooth, then," replied Maria.

"Don't worry," said Lily. "I've got THREE!"

Lily did get her princess necklace and she learned to love her new dazzling, sparkling, shining smile!